123 SESAME STREET®

RHYMING RAPUNZEL

Do NOT learn these words: rhyme, climb, cheese, please— and adorable!

Adapted from the original story by Jodie Shepherd

LEVEL 1 READER

READING LEVEL

Published by Dalmatian Press, LLC. All rights reserved.
Printed in Luogang, Guangdong, China.

The DALMATIAN PRESS name is a trademark of Dalmatian Publishing Group,
Franklin, Tennessee 37068-2068. 1-866-418-2572. DalmatianPress.com
No part of this book may be reproduced or copied in any form without written permission
from the copyright owner. CE16396/0113

Once upon a time,
there was a princess
named Rapunzel.
Rapunzel liked words.
And she *loved* words
that rhyme, like time,
and lime, and—rhyme!

But there was also a witch
who did NOT like rhymes.
She locked the princess
in a very, *very* tall tower.

Each day the witch came
to feed Rapunzel.

"Some cheese?" said the witch.

"Oh, please!" said the princess.

"Stop rhyming!" yelled the witch.

Rhyming Rapunzel was in
that tower for so very long,
that her hair grew very, *very* long!

One day Rapunzel sadly said,
"This tower is tall
and my window is small.
If I go down this wall,
I may land in a fall.
I hope someone bravely
will come by to save me!"

Then Rapunzel saw a prince
riding by on his horse.
She called, "Oh, me, oh, my!
I spy a prince going by!
Prince, come near!
Prince, come here!"

The prince looked up and said,
"What a cute and adorable lady!
Hello, I am Prince Grover!"

"Oh, please, come over!"
yelled Rapunzel.
"Princess Rapunzel is my name.
I am *so* glad that you came!"

The prince called up, "Rapunzel, please come down and play!"

"I can't. A witch locked me away," said Rapunzel.

"Hmmm," said Prince Grover. He looked at Rapunzel's very, very, *very* long hair and called, "Rapunzel, Rapunzel, let down your long hair!"

Rapunzel smiled and said, "Prince Grover, Prince Grover, how about a . . ."

"Chair?" said Prince Grover.
"No. I want to get up there,
but I cannot climb a chair.
Rapunzel, Rapunzel,
let down your long hair."

And Rapunzel let down a . . .

"Bear?" said Prince Grover.
"No, no. I want to
get up there,
but I cannot climb
a chair or bear.
Rapunzel, Rapunzel,
let down your long hair."

And Rapunzel let down a . . .

"Pear?" said Prince Grover.
"No, no, NO!
  I want to get up there,
  but I cannot climb a chair
  OR a bear OR a pear.
  No and no and NOPE!"

"Why not climb the rope?"
Rapunzel said sweetly.

So Prince Grover
began to climb.

until. . .

up

up

up

up

up

up

up

He went up

"Hello," said Prince Grover.
"It is not very nice to lock
a princess in such a tall tower.
How can we get away?"

"Prince, it was my hope
to just go down the rope,"
the princess said.

"Oh . . . yes!"
said Prince Grover.

So the prince and princess
went down. . .

down

down

down

down

down

to the ground—where they
soon spotted THE WITCH!

"Quick! Run and hide!"
said the prince.

"No! Let us ride!"
said Rapunzel.

"On my horse?"
said the prince.

"Well, of course!"
said Rapunzel.

And so the brave Prince Grover
and the adorable Rhyming Rapunzel
rode far, far away from that tall wall.

"And that's all!" called Rapunzel.